WHO STOLE MR. T?

LEILA & NUGGET MYSTERY #1

DESERAE & DUSTIN BRADY

CONTENTS

1. The Abominable Snow Dog   1
2. Turtlenapped   9
3. The Wicked Witch of West 73rd Street   19
4. Private Eye   29
5. Smudge   39
6. The A-Team   51
7. Spies   61
8. Weirdy Beardy   67
9. Turtle Soup   77
10. Thunk   85

OTHER BOOKS
BY DUSTIN BRADY

Trapped in a Video Game: Book One
Trapped in a Video Game: Book Two
Trapped in a Video Game: Book Three
Superhero for a Day: The Magic Magic Eight Ball

ACKNOWLEDGMENTS

Special thanks to April Brady for the cover and interior illustrations. You can follow April's artwork on Instagram: @aprilynnart.

THE ABOMINABLE SNOW DOG

POOMF!

Kait laughed as her friend Leila's dog Nugget dove headfirst into the snow again. "That's soooo funny! He acts like he's never seen snow before!"

"It snowed a few times last year, but I don't think he remembers," Leila said. "He was just a puppy."

Nugget pulled his head out of the snow pile and looked at Leila and Kait. His face was one big snowball.

"He's the Abominable Snow Dog!" Kait giggled.

Leila had to laugh. Nugget did look funny. "Come on Mr. Abominable," she said. "We'll never finish our walk if you keep this up."

Nugget tilted his head at Leila, thought about what she'd said for a second, and — POOMF! — dove again.

"I think Nugget likes snow days even more than we do, and he doesn't even go to school!" Kait said.

Leila wasn't too sure about that. She hadn't been able to think about anything except for what she'd do on her snow day ever since she'd first heard about the possibility of a storm earlier that week. Leila never paid attention to the news when her parents watched, but the second the weather guy had said "snow," her head popped up from her book like Nugget's does whenever he hears the word "treat."

"Did he say something about a snowstorm?" Leila asked.

"Eight to twelve inches in some parts of the viewing area," TV weather guy said.

"Eight to twelve inches?!" Leila squealed.

"Don't count your chickens before they're hatched," Leila's mom warned.

Oh, the chickens would be counted. That week, the only thing that Leila and all the other students in Mrs. Pierce's third-grade class could talk about was their snow day plans. A lot of kids were going to the Memphis Road sledding hill. A few wanted to make money by shoveling driveways. The Heather Lane crew — Leila, Kait and their friend Javy — were going to have a snowball fight and build an igloo and make homemade snow cones and pull each other around on sleds and then maybe build a snowman or at least a snow dog. It was going to be quite a day.

The night before the big day, Leila's mom warned her about getting too excited. "They're always wrong about the weather, you know," she said.

"I know," Leila replied.

"It hasn't even started snowing yet."

"I know."

"Just plan on going to school tomorrow. That way it'll be a nice surprise if you get off."

"I know."

"Goodnight, Leila."

"Night mom."

Leila's mom shut off the light, and Leila lay awake for an hour thinking about how great the snow day would be. She finally drifted off to sleep, and the next thing she knew, something small and furry was rolling all over her bed.

"Nugget!" Leila's dad hissed. "Get down! Sorry honey, I just took him out, and…"

Leila didn't hear the rest because she'd just felt the dog with her hand. He was wet. And cold. She opened her eyes to see

Nugget's snow-covered face two inches from her nose. "Is it a snow day?!" Leila interrupted.

"It's 6:15 in the morning," Leila's dad said with a smile.

"IS IT A SNOW DAY?!"

"Yes, it's a snow day. Now why don't you go back to bed?"

Leila picked up Nugget and danced around her room. "Snow day! Snow day! Snow day!" Nugget licked her face, then ran to the heat vent to get warm. Leila couldn't fall back asleep because today was a snow day and snow days are the best days. She ran downstairs an hour before she'd normally wake up, devoured breakfast, then read a mystery book until her mom said it was OK to call Kait.

"Did you hear?!" she shouted into the phone.

"YES!" Kait yelled back.

"Call Javy!" Leila said. "I'll bring Nugget to your house, and then we'll walk to Javy's."

Leila and Kait had gotten about ten steps into their walk before Nugget started his snow-diving routine. At this pace, they'd never get to Javy's.

"It's OK," Kait said. "Javy might not even be awake yet. He didn't answer the phone."

"Why wouldn't he answer the phone?!" Leila asked. "Doesn't he know how much we have to do today?"

Kait stopped and stared at a piece of paper taped to a telephone pole. "Oh no," she said.

"What is it?" Leila asked as she leaned in to read the sign. "Ohhhh noooooooooo."

"MISSING!" the sign said over a picture of a turtle.

NAME: MR. T
REWARD: ALL MY MONEY ($15.75)
CALL: 216-509-2212
ASK FOR JAVY MARTINEZ

2
TURTLENAPPED

Javy reached his house the same time Leila, Kait and Nugget did.

"Javy!" Kait yelled when she saw him. "What happened to Mr. T?!"

Javy slumped his shoulders and looked down. Nugget eyed the leftover fliers in his hand. "I don't know," Javy said. "I haven't seen him since I woke up this morning."

Nugget jumped and grabbed one of the fliers. He started wagging his tail, waiting for Javy to chase him. Javy just looked sad. Nugget stopped wagging his tail.

"Don't worry! We'll help you find him!" Kait said. "Right, Leila?"

"Oh, uh, yeah of course!" Leila said, a little worried about what this search might mean for the snowball fight.

"Really?" Javy asked. "That's great you guys! Come in." Javy opened the door and — *CRASH!* — knocked over a pile of boards inside the kitchen. "Yipes!" he said. "I'm so sorry!"

A construction worker with a big, wooly beard shook his head and helped Javy pile the boards back up. "My parents are getting the kitchen remodeled today," Javy explained to Leila and Kait as he finished stacking. "We'll have to be careful in here."

The kids picked their way through the maze of tools and wood until they got to a side room attached to the kitchen. "Here's Mr. T's winter home," Javy said.

Javy's family had turned their pantry into a turtle paradise. The walls were covered with pictures of Javy's family posing with Mr. T and drawings of the turtle dressed in funny costumes. A

11

wooden box piled high with dirt and
moss took up every inch of floor space.
The box held a small pool, a heat lamp, a
few rocks and logs, but no turtle.

"What do you think happened?" Leila
asked.

Javy looked at the two workers in the
kitchen and lowered his voice. "Come to

my room, and I'll tell you," he said.

The kids kept their boots on until they reached the dining room so they wouldn't get soggy socks from all the snow that had been tracked into the kitchen, then they turned into Javy's room. As soon as Nugget saw the carpet, he started pushing himself all over the floor to dry himself off. Kait started to take off her coat before thinking better of it. "It's cold in here," she said.

Javy nodded. "My dad likes to see how late in the year he can go without turning the heat on," he said. "He must be trying to beat his record."

"So when was the last time you saw Mr. T?" Leila asked, eager to find this turtle so they could get back on schedule with the snow day plans.

Javy plopped onto his bed. "Last night, he was in his home. I said goodnight and went to sleep. When I woke up this morning — poof! He was gone! I looked all over the house, but he's nowhere."

"What do you think happened?" Kait asked.

"I think he escaped," Javy said. "Sometimes we let him out so he can walk around the house. But when you do that, you've got to keep an eye on him. The construction guys have been going in and out of the house ever since they got here early this morning. I think they left the door open, and Mr. T ran away." Javy buried his head between his knees.

Kait moved closer and tried to make Javy feel better. "I mean, Mr. T is a turtle," she said with a smile. "He probably didn't *RUN* anywhere."

Javy sniffed a few times. "You know what I mean. I just don't know why he would want to leave in the first place. He hates the cold!"

Leila sat up. Javy had just reminded her of the book she'd been reading earlier that morning — *The Ice Cold Case*. It was a mystery that took place at a frozen pond (she'd picked it out in honor of the snow day). The detective in the book figured out that the thief was a raccoon by following prints in the snow. "If Mr. T went outside, we should be able to follow his tracks in the fresh snow, right?" Leila asked.

Javy perked up. "Oh yeah! That's a great idea!"

Leila left Nugget in the room so he wouldn't mess up the tracks, then led the way to the side door. She was feeling great about her plan until she looked down. The snow by the door was almost packed solid with footprints from the kids, the workers and Javy's parents. There was no way they could find turtle tracks in this mess. "Let's follow some of these away from the house where the snow isn't so packed," Leila suggested.

The biggest clump of tracks went down the driveway, so the kids followed those first. Unfortunately, they all ended at the bright red construction van parked at the end of the driveway. Next, they got excited when Kait spotted paw prints cutting across the front yard, but then Leila reminded everyone that's where they'd just walked with Nugget. Finally, they followed a set of prints that Javy guessed belonged to his dad going to the garage, but they didn't find any turtle tracks that way either.

"That's it," Javy said. "He must have gotten out before it started snowing. That was a good idea though, Leila."

"Bark! Bark!" Nugget had just spotted the kids through the bedroom window, and he seemed real upset that he hadn't been invited to the search party. He pressed his face up to the window, making a heart-shaped fog with his nose.

"OK, OK, we're coming," Leila said as she walked toward the window.

Kait, who'd been following close behind, grabbed Leila's arm. "Leila! Look!" She pointed to a single set of suspicious footprints that walked through Javy's backyard, to the back patio door, then left again into the neighbor's yard.

"Javy," Kait said. "What if Mr. T didn't run away at all?"

"What do you mean?" Javy asked.

Kait's eyes were wide. "What if he got turtlenapped?!"

3

THE WICKED WITCH OF WEST 73RD STREET

Kait gasped. "If Mr. T got turtlenapped, then this is a real-life mystery!" she exclaimed. Kait was trying to hide her excitement about the idea of a mystery in front of Javy, but the sparkle in her eyes gave her away.

Javy looked down. "I don't care about a mystery," he said. "I just want my friend back."

"Oh, we'll get him back," Kait said. "You know why? Because you're standing next to the best detective in town."

Javy looked up, surprised. "Leila?" he asked.

Leila gave Kait a weird look. "Detective? What are you talking about?"

Kait ignored her. "Leila's read basically every mystery book, so she knows all the tricks. Just the other day, she helped me solve the mystery of my missing Halloween candy."

"I reminded you that you ate it all," Leila said.

"See, isn't she good? She'll catch the turtlenapper before lunchtime!"

"Could you?" Javy asked hopefully.

Leila knew she was no detective, but she did very much want to find Mr. T in time to at least build an igloo. "We'll do our best," Leila said.

Kait squealed. "What do we do first?!"

Leila looked at the suspicious footprints. "We should probably follow these, right?"

"See?" Kait said to Javy. "Just like a real detective!"

The gang followed the footprints from Javy's back door, through the yard, past a row of bushes and into the neighbor's yard. Javy stopped when he saw which house the tracks had come from. "Mrs. Crenshaw." He shook his head. "I should have known."

"She doesn't like Mr. T?" Leila asked.

Javy pointed to the row of bushes they were standing next to. "These are Mrs. Crenshaw's rose bushes," he said. Then he pointed to a short wire fence next to the bushes. "And that's Mr. T's summer home. Every year, Mr. T figures out a way to eat half of Mrs. Crenshaw's roses through his pen, and every year she gets sooooo mad."

Leila scrunched up her face. "Mad

enough to break into your house and steal your pet?" she asked. "That's pretty mean."

"Oh, she's mean all right," Kait said. "SO mean! Remember that business I started a couple years ago? The one where I sold cool fall leaves?"

Leila remembered Kait's grandma giving her a quarter for some leaves Kait had found, which is not exactly a business, but she didn't argue. "I remember," Leila said.

"Well, Mrs. Crenshaw yelled at me for picking leaves off her tree! Can you believe it?"

"It is her tree," Leila pointed out.

"It was the FALL!" Kait exclaimed. "They were going to FALL off in a couple days anyways. She's like a witch, she's so mean!"

"That's not nice to say about

someone," Leila said. "It just sounds like she wants to keep her trees nice."

"Yeah, so she can use them for witch things," Kait mumbled.

"I wouldn't say she's a witch," Javy said, "But she's lived behind us ever since I was little, and I don't think she's come over even once. Don't you think it's suspicious that she shows up the very morning that Mr. T goes missing?"

Leila had to admit that it did seem odd.

"So how are we going to catch her?" Kait asked. Then her eyes lit up. "Do we get to spy?!"

Leila knew how much Kait loved spying on people, but she had a better idea. "How about we just ask her?" she said.

Kait made a face. "I'm not going over there," she said.

"Come on. I'll bring Nugget," Leila said.

Leila went back inside and got Nugget, who was more than happy to pounce in the snow again. Leila tugged on the leash to keep him moving. "Don't worry buddy," she said. "Soon we can play in the snow all we want." That gave her an idea. Maybe they could play in the snow and solve a mystery at the same time! She made a snowball and called Kait's name.

"What?" Kait asked as she turned around.

PIFF! It hit her square in the chest.

Kait giggled and threw a snowball at Javy. Javy did not join the fun. "Sorry guys. I wish I were in the mood to play, but I don't really feel like it right now. Why don't you two have a snowball fight, and I'll talk to Mrs. Crenshaw myself?"

Leila felt bad for taking Javy away from his search. "No Javy, we'll help you. Right Kait?"

Kait dropped the big, juicy snowball she'd been building. "Right. Of course."

Since Mrs. Crenshaw lived behind Javy and the kids felt she might get mad at them if they tromped through her backyard, they walked around the block to get to the front door.

"What do we say when we get there?" Javy asked.

"YOU'RE UNDER ARREST!" Kait yelled. "Then we handcuff her."

"We're not arresting anyone," Leila said. "Let's just ask her if she knows what happened to Mr. T."

"If she did take him, won't she just lie?" Javy asked as they rounded the corner onto W. 73rd St.

"If she tries to lie, she'll mess up and we'll catch her. That's what always happens in the books," Leila said, even though she had no idea how to catch someone in a lie.

"All I know is, if she answers the door riding on a broom, I'm running back home before she can get me," Kait said.

Leila rolled her eyes as she turned up Mrs. Crenshaw's driveway. "Be nice," she said. She scooped up Nugget right before they got to the door. She'd learned a long time ago that a small, waggly-tailed dog can make even the meanest adults nice.

Leila took a deep breath to gather her courage. The house was old and a little creepy. She stood in front of the door for a second and knocked. The door opened after just one knock, and a tall, skinny woman with straight, gray hair came to the door. She was holding a broom.

"What do you want?" she asked.

Kait stared at the broom for a moment before running off the porch.

PRIVATE EYE

Leila's face turned red. She did not expect her friend to be so embarrassing. "We're looking for his turtle," she finally said. "Can you help us?"

Mrs. Crenshaw looked at Leila and Javy, and then at Nugget, who even someone like Mrs. Crenshaw would have to admit looked pretty cute with his tongue sticking out. "Come in," she said.

"Oh no," Javy said. "It's OK, we were just…"

"Come in so I can close this door and stop letting all the heat out!" Mrs. Crenshaw snapped. Javy and Leila quickly stepped inside. "Take off your shoes," Mrs. Crenshaw instructed. They obeyed. "You two came at a good time. Can you hold this for me?" She handed Javy a dustpan.

"Oh, uh, sure," Javy said. While Javy helped Mrs. Crenshaw sweep the floor, Leila looked around. The house was brighter than she'd expected. Everything seemed to sparkle — especially the kitchen. She set Nugget down to explore. She knew she wouldn't be allowed to snoop around a stranger's house, but a cute, little doggy could get away with it. Maybe he'd find Mr. T or at least sniff out a clue. But as soon as Leila set him down, Nugget barreled for a tote bag in the kitchen. "Nugget!" Leila yelled after him. Too late. He'd already shoved his head and half his body inside, so when he looked at her, he was half-dog, half-bag.

"I'm sorry about my dog," Leila said as she ran over to Nugget. But before she could reach the bag, Nugget heard the heater turn on, shook off the bag and curled up in front of the vent.

Mrs. Crenshaw seemed to be losing patience with the two kids. "How can I help you?"

"We're looking for my pet turtle," Javy said. "Have you seen him?"

"Not since he finished off the last of my roses this summer," Mrs. Crenshaw answered flatly.

Javy's face turned red. "OK," he said as he turned to leave. "Thank you for your time."

Leila wasn't about to give up that easily. "This morning," she said. "Did you see him when you went to Javy's house this morning?"

That seemed to startle Mrs. Crenshaw, which made Leila happy. Good detectives are always startling people. "How did you know that?" Mrs. Crenshaw asked. "Were you spying on me?"

"Oh no!" Leila said. "I was just, uh, I mean…"

Javy jumped in. "Leila's a detective!"

he said.

That made Mrs. Crenshaw crack a small smile for the first time all morning. "A detective?"

Leila blushed. "Oh no, not really a detective. I mean, well you see, we just noticed footprints going from your house to Javy's back door. And so we were wondering what you were doing there this morning. That's all."

Mrs. Crenshaw tilted her head a bit, a full smile on her face now. "You followed footprints? That sure sounds like something a detective would do to me."

Leila blushed even redder if that were possible.

"Well," Mrs. Crenshaw said, "this morning, I recognized the red van in the Martinezes' driveway. It was the same company that helped me with my kitchen. Did you notice the name on the van?"

Leila shook her head.

"You need to pay attention to these things," Mrs. Crenshaw said. "That's what good detectives do. It's 'Margolis Construction.' Anyway, they did a good job on my kitchen, but they never took their shoes off and ended up tracking mud everywhere. It took me a week to scrub everything. I wanted to warn Mrs. Martinez so she wouldn't have the same problem."

"So you didn't take Mr. T?" Javy asked.

"No dear," Mrs. Crenshaw said. "That turtle and I are not friends, but I would never do anything like that."

"I know," Javy sighed. "I just really wanted to find him, and I thought maybe, I don't know…"

"It's OK," Mrs. Crenshaw said. "You've got to follow the clues. And I did actually see your turtle this morning."

"Really?!" Javy perked up.

Mrs. Crenshaw nodded. "While I was talking to your mom, I noticed your dad holding the turtle in the hallway."

"Oh wow!" Javy said. "Do you remember what time it was?"

"It was around 7:30."

"Thank you!" Leila said. "That's so helpful!"

"Aren't you going to write that down?" Mrs. Crenshaw asked.

"What do you mean?"

"It's a clue. You should write it down."

"Oh. Well, I don't really have pen or paper," Leila said.

Mrs. Crenshaw thought for a moment. "Let me get you something," she finally said. She walked upstairs, then came down a few minutes later with an old, hard-bound notepad that said "PRIVATE EYE" on the front. She flipped the crinkly pages until she found a blank one. "Why don't you use this?"

Leila wrote down a few clues from their conversation, then flipped through the book. It was filled with neat handwriting, a few drawings and lots of green check marks. "What is this?"

"When I was your age, I set up a detective agency in my neighborhood where I would solve cases for a nickel each. That was my detective notebook. I always knew how much money I'd made because each case I solved got a green check mark."

Leila flipped through the book again, counting all the check marks. "Wow! You were good!"

Mrs. Crenshaw allowed herself another smile. "To be honest, most of

my solutions came from books I was reading. Have you ever read Nancy Drew?"

"Of course!" Leila said. "All the ones at the library at least."

"I read all of them at least five times each," Mrs. Crenshaw said. Then she leaned in and raised an eyebrow. "I still have all of the originals if you ever want to borrow them."

"Wow!"

Mrs. Crenshaw turned back to Javy. "I'm sorry about your turtle," she said. "I know mysteries are no fun when you're the one who's lost a friend."

"We'll find him," Javy said.

Mrs. Crenshaw nodded. "Oh, I know you will. And when you do, we're going to teach him some rosebush manners!"

SMUDGE

Leila had her head buried in her notebook as she walked out of Mrs. Crenshaw's house. What could they be missing?

PIFF! A snowball hit her square in the face.

"Kait!"

"What?" Kait rejoined Leila and Javy from her hideout behind Mrs. Crenshaw's tree. "You wanted a snowball fight, right?"

"I'm trying to figure something out."

They walked in silence for a few seconds so Leila could think, then Kait whispered, "Did she try to cook you?"

"Excuse me?"

"The witch. Did she try to cook you?"

"OK, we can't be friends if you're going to keep calling people names," Leila said. "Her name is Mrs. Crenshaw. And in fact, she gave us an important clue. She saw Mr. T with Javy's dad at — let's see — 7:30 this morning."

"That's right before he leaves for work," Javy said.

"So your dad probably took the turtle to the vet or something on his way to work," Kait said.

Javy shook his head. "No way. I called him as soon as I woke up, and he didn't know where Mr. T was."

Kait looked at Javy out of the corner of her eye like she felt sorry for him, then said, "Well maybe… Never mind."

"What is it?" Javy asked.

"Well, what if he wasn't telling the truth?"

"Are you saying my dad would lie to me?"

"You're right, you're right. I'm sure he didn't. I barely even know your dad. He seems nice."

Leila shot a mean look at Kait. "Why would you say something like that?"

"Well, it's just… OK, one time my cousin Clara told me a story. You know my cousin Clara?"

Leila nodded. Cousin Clara was the one with all of the hard-to-believe stories.

"OK, well one time Clara told me about her friend Olivia who had a bunny named Smudge. She named him Smudge because he had a black smudge between his eyes that looked like someone had tried to erase something from his forehead. Anyways, Smudge was a great bunny, except he pooped everywhere. Like *EVERYWHERE*. And you know that bunny poops look kind of like chocolate candies and Olivia had a 2-year-old brother and…"

"I don't understand what this gross poo story has to do with Mr. T," Javy interrupted.

"I'm getting there," Kait said. "So one day, Smudge disappears. Olivia looks everywhere, but she never finds him. She figures he's run away and gives up looking. Then, a couple weeks later, she goes to Lake Farm Park — that's the field trip you go on in second grade where they let you milk the cow."

"We know," Leila said. Like Javy, she was also getting impatient with this story.

"Well sitting right next to the goats is a bunny rabbit that had a black smudge between his eyes. Turns out, it's Olivia's bunny. She finds out that her parents had gotten mad at the bunny and decided to give it away to the farm without telling her."

Javy looked horrified. Leila just shook her head. "So you're telling us the parents gave the bunny away because it pooped a lot? Couldn't they have just kept it in the cage more?"

Kait shrugged. "I mean it was pooping or chewing stuff or something. I forget exactly, but the point is the bunny was being bad, so her parents gave it away without telling her."

Javy was getting upset. "My dad would never give away Mr. T! He — he's been part of the family my whole life!"

Kait shrugged. "So was Smudge."

"You're not helping," Leila hissed at Kait. Then she turned to Javy and tried to calm him down. "That story probably wasn't true. Kait's cousin makes stuff up all the time. Let's focus on what we know. We know Mr. T was in the house at 7:30, right?"

Javy stopped panicking for a second to nod.

"And we know that there aren't any turtle tracks leaving the house, right?"

Javy nodded again.

"So he's probably still in the house!"

"Unless…"

That was all Kait could get out before Leila talked over her. "Why don't we all go back to the house and look for Mr. T again?"

Javy nodded. "That's a good idea. We can look for Mr. T until my dad comes home for lunch; then we can ask him what else he knows." While they walked back to the house, they decided that Javy would search the bedrooms, Kait would tackle the bathrooms and office, while Leila would take the living room and kitchen. "What about Nugget?" Javy asked. "Don't police use dogs to find missing people sometimes? Maybe Nugget can sniff out Mr. T?"

Leila looked at Nugget, who was jumping at falling snowflakes. "I don't think Nugget is that type of dog."

Javy wouldn't give up on his Nugget idea. When they got back to the house, he ran to Mr. T's home. "This is what the police do," Javy explained. "They have the dog sniff something from the missing person, so they know what they smell like." Then he paused. "Huh," he said.

"What is it?" Leila asked.

"I was going to have Nugget sniff Mr. T's cave — it's an upside down flowerpot that he likes to crawl into — but it's gone."

"Let's just start looking in our rooms," Leila suggested. Everyone agreed that would be best, and they split up. Leila started in the living room with Nugget. Nugget did a great job of searching the room, mostly because he was looking for snacks the whole time. He shoved his nose between cushions, squeezed behind the TV cabinet and Army crawled underneath the chair. No Mr. T, but they did find 57 cents in loose change, some goldfish snacks and a checker.

The kitchen was a little tougher because of all the construction, but Leila asked one of the workers for help. The guy with the beard seemed mean, so she asked one with a neck tattoo. He turned out to be nice. He moved boxes and opened cabinets for her, but they still couldn't find Mr. T. Fifteen minutes later, the kids met back in the living room. "Nothing," Leila said.

Javy was now wearing a too-big winter hat that covered half his head, making him look especially mopey. "I just found this hat. Are you guys cold too?"

Kait shook her head.

Leila wasn't about to give up. "How about the basement?"

"Mr. T doesn't walk down stairs," Javy said.

"But you never know!" Leila said. "We've got to check everywhere for clues!"

Javy shrugged, and they all walked downstairs. There wasn't much to Javy's basement. A washing machine and dryer stood against one wall, and tool shelves lined another. There were cleaning supplies in the corner, an old ping-pong table covered in boxes taking up the middle of the room, and that was about it. Leila walked around once, then started back up the stairs. Javy stopped her.

"Wait," he said. He walked to the ping-pong table and slowly pulled something out of a box. It was Mr. T's flower pot cave. He then took the box off the table and started sorting through it. It held all of Mr. T's possessions — food, toys, bowl, everything. It was exactly the type of thing someone would pack before giving away a turtle.

Just then a screen door closed upstairs.
Javy's dad had come home for lunch.

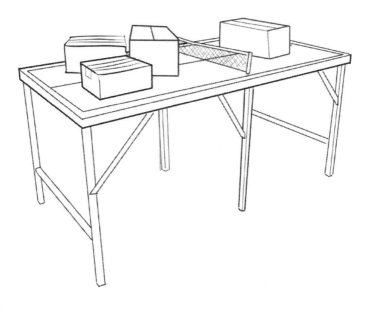

6

THE A-TEAM

Javy ran up the stairs with tears in his eyes. "DAD!" he yelled. "DAD, HOW COULD YOU?!"

"I told you," Kait said to Leila as she turned to follow Javy up the stairs.

"Save it," Leila mumbled.

Upstairs, Mr. Martinez had Javy wrapped in his arms. Nugget had also squeezed himself between the father and son, trying to get a free hug. "What's wrong?" Mr. Martinez kept asking.

"He was a good turtle!" Javy said between sobs. "He was such a good turtle! How could you give him away?"

"Give him away? I didn't give him away!" Mr. Martinez said. He looked at Javy, then at Leila and Kait. "Why would you even think that?"

"We followed the clues!" Kait said proudly.

"Clues? What clues?"

Javy laid out all the clues for his father the best he could between tears. "There aren't any turtle tracks outside (*sob*), and Mrs. Crenshaw saw you holding Mr. T this morning (*sob*), and then you packed all his stuff in a box to give away (*sob*)."

"Oh Javy," Mr. Martinez said. "I would never give Mr. T away. You know that."

"But the box…"

"I packed his stuff to keep it safe during the construction," Mr. Martinez said.

"But you're the only one who left the

house," Kait said. "And Mr. T isn't here, so you had to have taken him somewhere."

Mr. Martinez seemed annoyed for a second that the neighbor girl kept accusing him of lying, but he could see how upset this was making Javy. He took a breath and slowed things down a bit. "Javy, have I ever told you how Mr. T got in this family?"

Javy shrugged. "You got him a long time ago, right?"

"Not just a long time ago. I got him when I was exactly your age."

Leila gasped. "But that means that Mr. T must be…" she trailed off.

"Old?" Mr. Martinez offered.

Leila blushed.

"Mr. T is actually 32," Mr. Martinez said. "That's a pretty old pet, huh?"

Leila nodded.

"In third grade, I had a teacher named Mrs. Stanley. Mrs. Stanley was my favorite teacher ever, mostly because she kept a family of turtles right there in the classroom. She nicknamed the turtles the A-Team after the TV show."

Everyone stared blankly at Mr. Martinez.

"The A-Team? You guys know the A-Team, right? They'd make like flamethrowers out of gas pumps and... You know what? It's not important. The important thing is that Mrs. Stanley had a rule where if you got an "A" on your homework, you got to help feed the A-Team that day. I wasn't always the best student, but I loved those turtles so much that I worked extra hard and crushed my homework that year. One turtle in particular was my favorite."

"Mr. T?" Javy asked.

Mr. Martinez nodded. "We started doing this thing where I would hold the food up in the air, and he would jump for it. He wouldn't do it for anyone else — just me."

"His jump trick?" Javy asked. "I thought all turtles did that."

"It's very rare," Mr. Martinez said. "Anyways, I started coming in early and staying late just to hang out with Mr. T. Mrs. Stanley must have noticed how much I'd bonded with the turtle because she took me aside one day after school and asked if I'd like to keep him. I was so excited that I dragged my mom to the store that night so we could buy every turtle toy they had. I don't think I slept for three nights. I just stayed up imagining all the adventures I'd have with Mr. T. Well, the day finally arrived when I was supposed to take Mr. T home. It was the last day of school before Christmas break. I showed up to school with a box that had Mr. T's name on it. Only he was gone."

Kait gasped.

"That's how I felt too," Mr. Martinez said. "Mrs. Stanley said that she'd been cleaning the cage that morning, and he just disappeared. She had the whole class search for Mr. T, but nobody found him. After a few hours, everybody else had forgotten about him. We had a party and watched a movie. It was the A-Team holiday special, which made me feel even worse. I remember that the heat was broken that day, so we all wore our coats in the classroom. I buried my head in my coat like a turtle and cried through the whole movie."

For the first time that day, Leila thought about how she'd feel if she ever lost Nugget. She decided that it must be the worst feeling in the world. "So what happened?" she asked.

"We never found him. The end-of-the-day bell rang, and I walked out of class behind a kid named Manny. Manny was part of the AV Club, which meant he helped the teacher wheel in the TV and hook up the video. I remember walking slowly as Manny pushed the TV cart and noticing that his video equipment bookbag looked weird. It had a big bulge in it. I looked closer. Then it started squirming. Manny's desk was next to mine because our last names were so close, and I remembered how jealous he'd been that I was getting Mr. T. I ran and got Mrs. Stanley, we opened the bookbag, and sure enough, there was Mr. T.

Kait gasped again. "Did you have him arrested?!"

"You know what? I couldn't get mad at him. He wouldn't even admit to taking the turtle, but I didn't care. That's how happy I was to have my buddy back." Then Mr. Martinez looked at his son. "Javy, I know how it feels to lose a best friend. Believe me, I'd never do that to you."

Javy hugged his dad. "I know, Dad."

During the hug, Leila brought out her detective notebook to write down a few more clues.

- A-Team
- Mrs. Stanley
- Manny

She paused and looked up. "Mr. Martinez, what was Manny's last name?"

"Margolis," he said.

Leila froze and stared at the first clue she'd written at the top of the page. She couldn't believe it. She may have just solved the case.

SPIES

"You OK?" Kait whispered to Leila. "You look like you're gonna hurl."

"I think I just solved the case," Leila whispered. "We need to talk to Javy. Alone."

"Hey Javy," Kait stuck her face between Javy and his dad. "You want to show us those snow fort plans now?"

"What snow fort plans?" Javy asked. "This is no time for a snow fort! We need to…"

Kait grabbed Javy's arm and started dragging him away. "They're in your room, right? Let's go!" Javy tried to push off, but Kait had a vice grip. "Don't wait for us, Mr. Martinez!" she said. "I know you've got to eat your lunch and get back to work! Yum yum!"

"Yum yum?" Leila asked when Javy's door closed behind them.

"Snow fort?!" Javy yelled. "I told you two — if you want to play in the snow, that's fine. But this is important to me! So you can…"

"Hush," Kait interrupted. "We just needed to get you in here. Leila solved the case."

Javy's eyes got wide.

"And just so you know, this is important to us too," Leila said. "I mean, I was really looking forward to the snow day, but you're my friend, and now I want to help you get Mr. T back more than anything."

"Thank you, Leila," Javy said. "Now

what did you find?"

Everyone's eyes were on Leila. Even Nugget had jumped onto the bed and was staring at her. She suddenly got a chill. "I, well, actually I'm pretty cold."

Kait threw Leila a blanket. "Just spit it out!" she said.

Leila wrapped up and settled down. "It's the first clue I wrote down," she said. "Look." She turned around her notebook to show Javy and Kait the name on the red van outside of Javy's house — **Margolis Construction.**

"Okayyyyy," Javy said.

"Manny's last name was Margolis," Leila explained.

Kait gasped. "The turtlenapper is back to finish the job!"

"But why would my dad hire Mr. Margolis if he knows he's a turtlenapper?" Javy asked.

"That's what I've been trying to figure out," Leila said. "Maybe it's a different Margolis."

Javy shook his head. "I don't think so. I heard my dad speaking Spanish with another man early this morning. I couldn't hear everything they were saying, but from the way they were talking, it sounded like they'd grown up together."

Kait held up her hand. "What about this — we know Mr. Margolis is a criminal, right? Maybe your dad hired him to help him pay for his crimes. Then your dad saw Mr. Margolis steal Mr. T this morning, but Mr. Margolis pulled out a gun and told him not to say anything!"

Javy, Leila and Nugget stared at Kait confused. Even for Kait, that was a pretty crazy idea. Finally, Leila spoke up. "Javy, I don't know why your dad trusts Mr. Margolis, but whatever the reason, I think it's up to us to catch him."

"But how?" Javy asked. "Do we question him?"

"NO!" Kait shouted. "WE SPY!"

Leila sighed. "I hate to say it, but Kait might be right this time. I think we need to spy."

Kait pumped her fist. "Yes! OK Javy, we need binoculars and a listening device. If you don't have a real spy listening device, a glass cup should do. Now, do you…"

Leila stopped Kait right there. "No

binoculars," she said. "We need to get close enough to search their stuff."

Kait folded her arms across her chest. "Well, I only do far-away spying."

"Bark! Bark!" Everyone turned to Nugget. He was standing on the edge of the bed, wagging his tail. "Bark!"

Javy laughed. "Nugget looks like he's ready to help."

Leila nodded. "And I think I know just the way."

8
WEIRDY BEARDY

The kids waited until Javy's dad was ready to go back to work.

"Javy, I'm leaving!" Mr. Martinez shouted from the kitchen. "Do I get a hug goodbye?"

Kait slapped Javy on the shoulder, and he marched to the kitchen. Leila, Kait and Nugget waited in the bedroom while Javy said goodbye to his dad and then secretly scattered chunks of string cheese throughout the kitchen. A minute later, he came back to the room and nodded. Leila then whispered Nugget's three favorite words into the dog's ear. "Find the treats!"

Nugget tore out of the room and sprinted through the house until he found the first chunk of cheese in the dining room. He leaped over a pile of tile on the ground and continued his search inside the kitchen. "I'm so sorry!" Kait said to the startled workers who had to pause what they were doing when a small, furry bullet bounded over them and started sniffing everything in sight.

The three kids ran through the room, pretending to chase Nugget while they really searched every nook and cranny for signs of turtlenapping.

"Nugget, come back!" Javy yelled while he poked his head into a toolbox.

"You're not being a good dog!" Leila said as she opened a cabinet. She made sure to yell the "good dog" part of the sentence extra loud so Nugget knew he was doing a great job.

Kait flipped a cardboard box upside down, dumping out covers for power outlets and heater vents. "I can use this box to catch him!" she announced. When she found nothing interesting inside, she moved onto another box. *Dump*. "Or maybe this would be better!"

The two workers (whom Kait had earlier nicknamed "Weirdy Beardy" and "Tattoo Tom") waited patiently while the little show in front of them finished up. When the kids finally decided that the turtle was no longer in the kitchen, Leila swooped Nugget into her arms and apologized to the workers. Time for Part Two of the plan.

For Part Two, the kids bundled up and went outside to build a snow fort. But this wasn't the fort they'd been planning for the last week. No, this would be their special base to sneak into the real target — the van. Once they finished the fort, Leila curled up with Nugget inside while Javy and Kait crouched nearby. For a few minutes, everything was silent. Leila's heart was pounding. This was the most exciting snow day she could have ever imagined!

At that moment, Weirdy Beardy walked out of the house toward the van. Leila took a sharp breath. This was it! Any second now, Kait should be starting a snowball fight with Javy. She'd hit him and run toward the van. Then Javy would throw a snowball back at her, but he'd throw it way over her head on purpose. When Javy would let go of the snowball, Leila would release Nugget, who'd chase the snowball into the van. Finally, the kids would follow Nugget into the van and find Mr. T. It was, they'd all agreed, the perfect plan.

PIFF!

"Ow!" Javy shouted. "Hey, you didn't need to throw it in my face," he muttered.

"Focus, guys," Leila hissed from her snow fort.

"Haha, can't catch me!" Kait ran

toward the van just as Weirdy Beardy opened its back door. Javy made a snowball, wound up and threw it at the van. "Go!" Leila said as she turned Nugget loose. Nugget got low to the ground and barreled after the snowball. Javy had thrown a perfect lob. The snowball was just about to land inside the van, when —

SLAM!

Weirdy Beardy closed up the van, and…

PIFF!

The snowball hit the back door. Nugget stared at the snow spot on the van and then looked back at Leila. Weirdy Beardy walked out the side of the van with a long, plastic tube under his arm.

Leila jumped out of her snow fort. "Oh no!" she shouted. Weirdy Beardy didn't even notice her as he walked into the house.

"What do we do now?" Javy asked.

"I, I don't know," Leila said as she picked up Nugget. "We could try it again when they come back out, but they'll be expecting it this time. Should we call the police? They probably won't come. Oh boy. Uh, well we could…"

While Leila's mind was spinning in circles, Kait calmly walked to the van's back door and opened it. "Coming?" she asked.

Leila and Javy stared with their mouths open.

"He didn't lock it. You should have noticed that, detective. Come on."

"I don't know," Leila finally said. "If Nugget goes in first, I feel like it's OK to chase him inside, but isn't this breaking into somewhere we don't belong?"

"How can it be breaking in? They're at Javy's house. You're allowed to look inside anything at your own house. It's the law." With that, she walked in. Javy looked at Kait, then back at Leila, then jumped into the van.

Leila didn't know much about the law, but she was almost positive that's not the way it works. She was just about to turn around when Nugget squirmed out of her arms and jumped into the van. "Nugget, wait!" She followed the dog inside but stopped short when she found Kait and Javy tearing through boxes and equipment. "Guys, come on," she said. "We shouldn't be doing this. Mr. T probably isn't even..." she stopped midsentence when her eyes landed on a small cooler with a turtle logo on it.

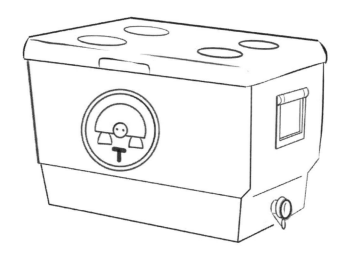

Javy gasped. "Mr. T!" he shouted. Before he could tear open the cooler, however, a figure appeared in the doorway.

"What are you kids doing in my van?!"

TURTLE SOUP

"AHHHHH!" Kait screamed.

"Hey, it's OK," the man said.

"AHHHHH!"

The man's expression changed from anger to concern. "Really, it's OK. I'm not going to hurt you."

"AH! AH! AHHHHHH!" Kait's face was turning red.

The man looked around nervously. "Come on, people are going to think I'm kidnapping you or something. Get out of the van, and we can talk in the house."

Kait instantly stopped screaming. "OK," she said as she climbed out.

Leila scooped up Nugget and nodded at Javy, who pulled his home's cordless phone from his coat pocket and made a quick call. When Leila hopped out of the van, she noticed a Margolis Construction pickup truck parked in the driveway that hadn't been there before. That must be where the man had come from.

Back in the house, the man sat across from the kids at the dining room table. "So now can you tell me why you were snooping in my van?"

Kait stuck her nose up in the air. "Only if you first tell us why you're stealing turtles."

"Wait, what are you talking about?"

Leila decided to jump in. "Are you Manny Margolis?"

"I am."

"You stole my dad's turtle in third grade," Javy shouted. "And you almost got away with stealing him again!"

"OK," Mr. Margolis held up his hand. "I've told your dad a million times — I did NOT steal that turtle in third grade."

Kait rolled her eyes. "Oh please. We're kids, but we're not stupid. It's pretty hard to not notice a giant turtle in your bookbag."

"Listen," Mr. Margolis said. "First of all, that wasn't my bookbag. That was the AV room bookbag, so I didn't know what was inside. Second, Mrs. Stanley was in the room with me the whole time I was setting up, so she would have noticed me stealing a turtle. Third..." Mr. Margolis shook his head. "I don't know why I'm explaining all this to you. You're not going to believe me now, just like no one believed me back then. Go ahead. Open the cooler and see for yourself."

Javy opened the cooler, looked inside, then slumped his shoulders. "It's soup," he said.

"Soup?!" Kait screeched. "You turned

Mr. T into soup?! YOU MONSTER!"

Weirdy Beardy popped his head into the dining room. "Is that my soup?" His eyes lit up when he saw the cooler in front of Javy. "Thanks! I was looking all over for this! I'm starving!" He grabbed the cooler and walked out of the dining room.

"I'm super sorry," Leila said.

"It's OK," Mr. Margolis said. "I just wish you would have talked to me rather than look through my stuff. There's some expensive equipment in there. Plus, breaking into someone else's vehicle is a crime, you know."

Leila shot Kait a glare. Then she looked around the room. "Has anyone seen Nugget?"

"Great!" Kait said. "Now we've got two missing animals? Does this house just eat pets?!"

"Here he is." Javy's dad walked into the room holding Nugget. "He was curled up in front of the living room heater." He gave Nugget to Leila and turned to Javy. "Now what's the big emergency that you had to call me home from work?"

"We thought Mr. Margolis had taken Mr. T, but we were wrong," Javy said.

"Why would you think he took Mr. T? Manny's one of my oldest friends!"

"Because he stole Mr. T when you were in third grade! We thought the only reason he'd be here is if he were finishing the job!"

Javy's dad shook his head. "You don't stay mad at someone forever just because they do something one time. You forgive people. Mr. Margolis was one of my best friends all through school. That's why I hired him to do our kitchen!"

"Well that was our last idea," Javy said. "We'll never find Mr. T now."

Something about this whole thing had been bothering Leila ever since Javy's dad had handed her Nugget. Finally, she realized what it was — Nugget was toasty warm. "Mr. Martinez," she said. "Has the heat been on all day?"

Javy's dad looked puzzled. "Of course. It's been on since last week. Why do you ask?"

Leila smiled. "I think I just solved two cases."

THUNK

Leila sprinted down the steps to Javy's basement while everyone else tried to keep up. "Leila, I told you — Mr. T can't walk down stairs!" Javy said.

"I know that," Leila replied. "He's not in the basement."

"What are you talking about?!" Kait asked.

Without answering, Leila grabbed a broom and looked at the ceiling. Javy's basement didn't have any ceiling tiles, which meant Leila had a clear view to all the pipes above. She walked across the room to where she guessed the kitchen

was and started banging pipes with the
handle of her broom.

CLANG!

She walked forward a step and banged
again.

CLANG!

She took another step and tried one
more time.

THUNK.

Leila tried twice more.

THUNK. THUNK.

"Why does it sound like that?" Javy asked.

Leila smiled. "Because there's a turtle in there!"

Javy's eyes got wide. "No way!"

"Let's go up to your bedroom and find out if I'm right!"

Nugget led the way by galloping up the stairs. Mr. Margolis grabbed a screwdriver from the kitchen and quickly unscrewed the heater vent from the bedroom wall. Javy reached inside. "Feel anything?" his dad asked.

"No," Javy said. Then he reached in a little farther. "Wait!" He leaned in as far as he could, smooshing his face against the wall. He gasped. "Mr. T!" He finally scooped out the turtle. Mr. T was a little dusty from the vent, but alive and looking quite pleased with himself.

"Mr. T, I can't believe you're OK!" Javy gave Mr. T a giant hug, or at least as big of a hug as he could give the turtle with Nugget squeezed in between.

"I'm so confused!" Kait said. "Did Mr. Margolis hide the turtle in there so he could take him later?"

"NO!" Leila and Mr. Margolis shouted at the same time.

"It was all Nugget," Leila explained while she petted her dog. "He loves curling up by the heater when he comes in from the cold. He's done it all day — at my house, in Mrs. Crenshaw's house and in the living room just now. I just remembered that the only place he hasn't done it is Javy's bedroom. That's because no heat has been coming out of the vent. Notice how cold it is in here compared to the rest of the house? Mr. T's been blocking the heat to this room all day!"

"But how did he get in there in the first place?" Javy asked.

"From the kitchen!" Leila was practically bouncing in place, she was so excited. "Your dad had to let Mr. T out of his turtle home this morning to put his stuff away when the construction guys came. Well, it got cold with them opening the door a bazillion times. We know Mr. T hates the cold — that's why he has a heat lamp and a flower pot cave in his home. So he went to the warmest cave he could find. Kait, do you remember what fell out of the first box you dumped in the kitchen this afternoon?"

Kait's eyes got wide. "The covers for the kitchen heater vents!"

Leila nodded. "So Mr. T crawled into

the duct and tried walking toward Javy's voice."

"I can't believe he was right here the whole time!" Javy said.

"You said you solved two mysteries," Mr. Margolis said. "Does that mean you figured out what happened to Mr. T when I was in third grade?"

Leila nodded. "Just like today, it was cold then too. Remember? The heat was broken. While the teacher was cleaning Mr. T's cage, he must have hidden in the warmest cave he could find."

"The bookbag!" Mr. Margolis exclaimed.

Javy's dad turned in shock. "So you really didn't steal Mr. T back then?!"

"That's what I've been telling you for the last 30 years!" Mr. Margolis said.

The two men did a complicated handshake and hugged. "I should have never doubted you," Javy's dad said.

"And I never should have toilet papered your house to get back at you for doubting me," Mr. Margolis said.

"That was you?!"

"That's THREE mysteries solved!" Kait exclaimed.

"Hey, does anyone know what time it is?" Javy asked.

Kait looked at her watch. "It's 3:30."

"Good."

"Why 'good'?" Kait asked.

"Because that leaves me two hours of daylight to get back at you for hitting me in the face with a snowball."

"You've got to catch me first!" Kait squealed as she ran out of the bedroom.

Nugget sprinted after her, excited to finally enjoy the snow day he'd been promised.

One week later, Leila was wiping

cookie crumbs off her face in Mrs. Crenshaw's kitchen as she wrapped up her story. "Mr. Margolis finished the kitchen remodel a few days later, and he even added some extra stuff to Mr. T's room to make it cooler," she said.

"That's wonderful," Mrs. Crenshaw said. "But you never finished your story. Did he ever catch her?"

"Did who catch who?"

"Did Javy ever catch up to Kait and get her back?"

"Oh yeah," Leila said. "We had the biggest snowball fight ever that afternoon! Toward the end, Javy used Nugget to lure Kait into a trap behind the shed, then he hit her with a snowball so big it could have been a snowman's head!"

Mrs. Crenshaw sat back and chuckled. "Good for him."

"Well anyways, here's your notebook back," Leila said as she slid the old "Private Eye" notebook across the table. "It was great."

"No no, I want you to keep it," Mrs. Crenshaw said. "You're the new detective on the block, now."

"Really?!" Leila asked. "I mean, I don't know if I'm really a detective."

"You don't know if you're a detective?" Mrs. Crenshaw asked. "Did you solve a case?"

"Well, yeah, but…"

"Then you're a detective. End of story. You don't need someone to give you a title for it to be true. Now, did you read any of the other cases in the notebook?"

"Oh! What? Uhhhh, I mean…" Leila wasn't normally a snooper like Kait, but if someone hands you a notebook full of real-life mysteries, what are you supposed to do?

"It's OK," Mrs. Crenshaw said. "You probably noticed that all of the cases had green check marks next to them except for one."

Leila had noticed. She flipped back to it. "The Case With No Clues." While most of the other cases in the book had just a handful of notes written underneath the title, this one had four whole pages of questions, maps, arrows and lots of scribbles.

Mrs. Crenshaw tapped the notebook. "Think you want to give this one a try?"

Leila stared at the title for a second, then looked up, confused. "There aren't any clues?"

"No clues," Mrs. Crenshaw said with a twinkle in her eye. "But there is a treasure.

AUTHORS' NOTE

Hope you had as much fun reading Leila and Nugget's adventure as we did writing it! We're hard at work on the second book right now. You can sign up to get a note when that book comes out, find pictures of the real Leila and Nugget and more at leilaandnugget.com.

If you liked this book, would you consider telling a friend or posting a short review on Amazon? We'd really appreciate the help!

Also, we'd love to hear from you! You can email us about anything at dustin@dustinbradybooks.com.

Thanks again for reading our book!

ABOUT THE AUTHORS

Deserae and Dustin Brady are the parents of Leila Brady (a baby) and Nugget Brady (a dog). They live in Cleveland, Ohio. Dustin wants to buy a turtle. Deserae does not.

ABOUT THE ILLUSTRATOR

April Brady is a professional illustrator in Pensacola, Florida. Deserae and Dustin feel lucky to have such a talented doggy-drawer as a sister-in-law.

Made in the USA
Lexington, KY
16 May 2019